BIG APPLE ™

A SASSY SURPRISE

WELCOME TO
BIG APPLE BARN!

BIG APPLE BARN™

A SASSY SURPRISE

by KRISTIN EARHART

Illustrations by
JOHN STEVEN GURNEY

A
LITTLE APPLE
PAPERBACK

SCHOLASTIC INC.
New York Toronto London Auckland Sydney
Mexico City New Delhi Hong Kong Buenos Aires

To Craig Walker, who wanted to see the world from a pony's perspective.
And to Jerry Wilson, whose 1983 prophecy came true.
Thanks for all the inspiration.

—*K.J.E.*

ISBN-13: 978-0-439-90095-9
ISBN-10: 0-439-90095-6

Text copyright © 2007 by Kristin Earhart.
Illustrations copyright © 2007 by Scholastic Inc.
SCHOLASTIC, LITTLE APPLE, BIG APPLE BARN, and associated logos are
trademarks and/or registered trademarks of Scholastic Inc.

12 11 10 9 8 7 6 5 4 3 2 1   7 8 9 10 11 12/0
40

Printed in the U.S.A.
First printing, January 2007

Contents

Chapter One

Another New Pony

Happy Go Lucky walked cheerfully down the aisle of Big Apple Barn. He breathed in the brisk, morning air. It was a beautiful day, and he had a good feeling he was headed outside! What more could a pony want?

Happy liked his life at Big Apple Barn. He had made lots of new friends there. Of all his new friends, Roscoe was his favorite. Roscoe was the barn mouse, and he was funny and clever and loyal.

Happy was now a school pony, so he had lots of new riders, too. Of all his new riders, Ivy was his favorite. Ivy was the younger daughter of Diane, the trainer. Ivy was sweet, smart, and kind.

Thanks to Ivy, Roscoe, and his other new friends, Happy thought his life was pretty good. Today was especially good, because today Ivy had come to get Happy out of his stall. She said she would take him for a special snack.

Ivy led Happy through the front doors of the main stables. Happy had been right. Ivy was taking him outside! Happy had not been outside in front of the stables since the day he arrived at Big Apple Barn, six weeks earlier. He didn't think it was nearly as scary now as he had then.

"Here you go, Happy," Ivy said. She sat down under an apple tree. "This patch of grass should be nice and sweet, just for you." Happy dropped his head down into the clump of grass, and Ivy reached out to pat his nose.

What could be better? Happy thought. He knew he was lucky to have Ivy. He and Ivy had worked hard to prove that they could be a good team, both in and out of the riding ring. Diane had said that Happy and Ivy were young, and they had a lot to learn about being a school pony and rider. But Diane agreed that they made good partners. She said they could help teach each other. It was just what they had wanted to hear!

"I have a surprise for you, Happy," Ivy announced.

Happy pricked his ears forward to listen to Ivy. *A surprise?* Happy thought. *I don't need another surprise. This grass is delicious. It is enough of a surprise!*

"Any minute now, and the surprise will be here," Ivy went on.

Happy continued to eat, pulling on tufts of spring-green grass with his teeth. *Yum!* Each bite seemed to melt in his mouth. With so much grass to eat, he wasn't very interested in Ivy's other surprise.

"I hope you like her," Ivy added.

Her?

Happy stopped eating and jerked his head up. *Her? What kind of surprise was Ivy talking about?*

"Mom couldn't stop talking about her," Ivy said. She tied a knot in a blade of grass. "She says this pony is just what the riding school needs."

So *that* was the surprise. Another new

pony was coming to Big Apple Barn! It was a pony for the riding school — and a *girl* pony at that. Happy thought about what this would mean. He had only been the new pony for a little more than a month. Now there would be someone else.

"It's so great!" Ivy said excitedly.

Happy took a deep breath and looked at his friend. Ivy had a smile on her face, and her eyes were warm. Happy lowered his head and blew into her wavy hair.

"Happy, stop it!" Ivy said with a giggle. She gently pushed his nose away. "That tickles."

Happy liked Ivy so much. But what if she liked the new pony better than him?

"Let's look for four-leaf clovers until they get here," Ivy suggested. She scooted over to a patch of clover near the trunk of the tree. Happy followed.

"I love four-leaf clovers," Ivy said, more to herself than to Happy. "You can wish on them. They're good luck, you know."

Happy had heard that before. But in his opinion, all clover was good. And a pony was lucky to find any clover, because it was tasty — three leaves, four leaves, five, six, or seven. Who cared? Happy nibbled at the little pink flowers and watched Ivy run her fingers through the clover patch.

Then Happy heard a low, rolling sound. He recognized it. That was the rumble of Diane's truck. Happy raised his head and looked down the road, past the white farmhouse. Sure enough, there was Diane's red-and-blue truck, with the trailer right behind it.

Ivy kept searching the clover while Happy turned around to watch the trailer.

The truck's wheels crunched along the gravel driveway and stopped close to the barn. When Diane slammed the driver's side door, Ivy looked up.

"Hi, Mom!" Ivy called.

"Hello, dear," Diane said with a wave.

"How's the new pony?" Ivy asked, getting up and standing alongside Happy.

"Fantastic!" Diane answered. Then she disappeared behind the trailer. Happy could hear the sound of the ramp being lowered. Happy and Ivy stood still and watched. It seemed like forever before they saw Diane again. When they did, she held a bright red lead line. She gave the line a light tug, and the new pony appeared behind her.

Happy took a short breath. The pony was about his height, and she was a stunning appaloosa. Most of her coat was a dark gray,

but her hips were bright white with black spots. Between her dark, sparkly eyes was a white star.

"Oh, she's beautiful," Ivy said with a sigh.

Happy agreed. He watched the appaloosa walk by. He realized he should whinny a hello to her, but by that time, Diane had already led the pony through the big barn doors.

Happy turned to Ivy. When Ivy looked back at him, she held out her hand.

"Look! I found a four-leaf clover," Ivy said. "Now I get to make a wish." She tightened her fingers around the clover and closed her eyes.

Happy looked from Ivy to the barn, where the new pony had just stepped out of view. He wondered what Ivy would wish for.

Chapter Two

Sassafras Surprise

After Diane had led the new pony into the barn, Ivy sat down and let Happy eat a little more grass. As he ate, he thought and thought.

When Happy had first come to Big Apple Barn, he had been nervous and scared. Everything at Big Apple Barn was big — much bigger than at his old home! Plus, Happy had never lived with other horses before, or been a school pony. He'd had no idea what to expect. There were lots of reasons why he had been anxious. But Happy did not think the new pony had looked nervous at all. She had held her head high and taken strong, sure steps. Then she had followed Diane right into the barn without even glancing around!

After a few minutes, Ivy walked Happy into the barn. Happy didn't mind being in the quiet of his stall again. It gave him some time to think.

But it didn't stay quiet for long. Pretty soon, Happy heard a light knocking sound. "Hey, Happy," a voice said. "Mind if I come in?"

"Hello, Roscoe," Happy answered. Happy watched as the head of the tiny gray mouse appeared over the top of his stall door. Roscoe pulled himself up with his front paws. He was gasping for breath.

Roscoe visited Happy every day, and Happy was relieved that Roscoe had come by at that moment. Happy could tell him all about the new pony, and then he could ask him what he thought. Roscoe always gave good advice.

"I ran all the way here," Roscoe announced, panting. "Guess what? There's a new pony at Big Apple Barn!"

Happy blinked. How did Roscoe already know about the new pony? She had just arrived!

"I just went to meet her," Roscoe said. "She's so nice! Her name is Sassafras Surprise, but she said that I could call her Sassy because she knows we'll be good friends."

Happy listened closely. Roscoe always got the barn news first. It was amazing! The mouse could easily scurry between stalls and find out what was going on. And it didn't hurt that Roscoe had a good nose for sniffing out gossip. It was a talent.

"Sassy came from another barn," Roscoe explained. "Her owner just moved to the city, so the girl had to sell Sassy."

"Oh, that's too bad." Happy felt awful for Sassy. He could not imagine how upset he would be if he ever had to leave Ivy. Happy was young, but he already knew how nice it was to find a rider who was a real partner and a true friend.

"Yeah," Roscoe agreed. "Sassy said she's a little nervous about being a school pony. She has never been one before."

Happy nodded. He knew what that was like. It had taken him a while to feel like a true school pony, too. Still, he was surprised that the new pony was concerned. She had seemed so sure of herself when she had stepped out of the trailer.

"You should see her, Happy," Roscoe said. "She's real pretty. She's got spots on her back, and she has one big star on her face." The mouse gave his head a quick shake, so his whiskers quivered. "You'll like her," he added.

Happy wasn't sure if he should tell Roscoe that he had already seen Sassy. Roscoe liked to be the first to see and hear things. "I was out front with Ivy when Sassy got here," Happy told his friend. When Roscoe didn't reply, Happy felt like he should say something else. "She is *pretty*."

"She is, isn't she?" Roscoe said. "I think all the lesson riders are going to want to ride

14

her. Ms. Diane did a good job, bringing Sassy to the barn."

Happy frowned. He was worried. He didn't care if *some* of the lesson riders wanted to ride Sassy, but there was one rider Happy wanted to keep for himself. Would Ivy choose to ride Sassy? Happy thought about asking Roscoe his opinion.

Happy looked over at his friend. Roscoe

was sitting by Happy's water bucket. The mouse was busy cleaning his whiskers, one by one. Then he dipped his tail in Happy's water. *Yuck!* Happy made a face, but he didn't say anything. Happy had never seen Roscoe primp like this before.

Roscoe fluffed up the white fur under his chin, and a sly smile spread across his face. When he looked around, he seemed surprised that Happy was watching him.

"What?" Roscoe questioned. "You have Ivy and other riders to groom you," he insisted. "A mouse needs to take care of himself! A mouse needs to look respectable."

Happy nodded. Roscoe made a good point. "You look cute," Happy told his friend.

Roscoe grimaced. "Cute?" he asked.

"Cute in a handsome way." Happy corrected himself quickly. How was he supposed to know that Roscoe was so sensitive?

"Good," Roscoe said. "That's what I was going for. Well, you were my first stop, Happy. I wanted to tell you about Sassy before anyone else. But now I have to make the rounds. I know everyone is going to be mighty curious about the new pony. It's up to me to get the word out."

"Thanks, Roscoe," Happy called. He decided he would ask Roscoe about Ivy when the mouse stopped by the next day. That would give him some time to think about it on his own first.

Chapter Three

An Introduction

The next day, Happy had just finished his morning grain when he heard steps coming down the barn aisle. He put his head over the stall door. To Happy's surprise, he saw a whole line of people and horses. Diane was in front, and Big Ben was walking next to her. Next came Andrea, Diane's older daughter, with Goldilocks. Happy pricked his ears forward when he saw that the last person was Ivy. Happy was about to nicker to her, but then he stopped. Ivy was leading Sassy.

Happy held his breath as the two walked by. Ivy didn't look at him. She was busy talking softly to the new pony, but the pony didn't seem to be listening. Instead, Sassy's dark eyes looked straight ahead. Sassy walked with the same high head and sure steps as she had the day before.

Happy watched as everyone headed out the barn door toward the pasture. He wondered if he would get to go to the field as well. Ivy usually took him to the pasture, and Happy was often turned out with Big Ben and Goldi. The tall, handsome chestnut and the short, caramel-colored pony were two of his best friends. Happy couldn't help wondering: Why hadn't Ivy taken him out, too? Why was she leading Sassy? Happy hoped Ivy had not forgotten him.

It wasn't long before Diane and Andrea returned to the barn. Happy neighed, so they would know that he wanted to go out. But Diane opened Cobalt's stall door, and Andrea headed toward Reggie's. Happy sighed as he watched Diane and Andrea put the lead lines on the other horses.

"What are you staring at, Happy?"

Happy spun his head around to see Ivy. She was standing nearby with a lead line in her hands.

"Don't you want to go out, boy?" Ivy asked.

Happy nickered. Of course he did! He was thrilled that Ivy had come back for him.

As Ivy led Happy outside, she talked to him like always. "Now, I want you to do me a favor," Ivy said. "I want for you to be nice to Sassy, the new pony. I think you two could be friends."

Friends with Sassy? Happy was willing to give it a try. He would do just about anything for Ivy. But when Ivy closed the gate behind him, Happy noticed that Sassy was not hanging out with Goldi and Big Ben. She was standing with Cobalt and Reggie, two young horses. Cobalt was a sleek black horse with a striking blaze on his face, and Reggie was a stocky dapple gray.

Happy got along with the other horses. He just wasn't completely comfortable with them. When Happy had first arrived at Big Apple Barn, Cobalt had given him some advice. It wasn't bad advice, but it hadn't worked for Happy. Since then, Happy had learned that he had a lot more in common with Big Ben and Goldi, even though they were much older than he was.

Still, Happy wanted to welcome the new pony, and not just because of Ivy. He knew it

was the polite thing to do. As he approached
the group, he noticed that Cobalt and Reggie
weren't even eating. They were both facing
Sassy, chatting away.

In the sunlight, Sassy was prettier than
ever. The dark gray that covered her head,
neck, and back glistened. The white on her
hips was perfectly clean, and her black spots
looked like they were painted on. As Happy

got closer, he noticed Cobalt glance in his direction. At once, the other horses' conversation came to a halt.

Cobalt and Reggie nodded a hello to Happy. Slowly, Sassy turned around to see why they had stopped talking. The new pony had a bright white star right between her eyes, and Happy couldn't help looking at it. He didn't mean to stare, but Happy had to admit it — this new pony was just lovely.

Happy searched for something to say, but he couldn't think of anything clever. "Hello, Sassy," he began. "I'm Happy."

The new pony tilted her head to the side. "It's nice to meet you, Happy," she replied. "But you should know, my full name is Sassafras Surprise." As she said this, she lifted her head, so she appeared slightly taller than Happy.

Happy gulped. Roscoe had told him that the pony's name was Sassafras Surprise, but Happy had only remembered her nickname. Happy had a full name, too. It was Happy Go Lucky. No one really called him that. If he went to shows one day, that would be the name he would use. But around the barn, Happy suited him just fine.

"I'm sorry," Happy stammered. "It's nice to meet you, Sassafras Surprise." He gave his tail a swish as he tried to think of something else to say. Then he remembered that Roscoe had mentioned that Sassafras Surprise was nervous about being a school pony. "You know," Happy continued, "Roscoe told me that you are going to be a school pony. I'm kind of new here, too, and I could tell you all about how the lessons work, if you want."

Then Cobalt stepped forward. "The fact

is," the horse remarked in his velvety voice, "that I've been here longer than you. You said it yourself, Happy. You're new." The black horse winked at Happy. "I have more experience, so I can be more helpful to Sassy."

"Oh," Happy said, "that's true. You have been here longer."

"Go on, ask me anything," Cobalt said, leaning toward the new pony.

"Um," she said, and then paused. "I haven't thought of any questions yet. But I'll be  sure to ask when I do. I appreciate the offer."

Happy looked from Cobalt to Reggie and then to Sassafras Surprise. "Well, I just wanted to say hello. And welcome to Big Apple Barn."

"That was nice of you, Happy," Sassafras Surprise replied.

Happy paused for a moment and looked the new pony in the eye. For a moment, she did not seem quite as sure of herself, but then she lifted her head again and tossed the mane out of her eyes.

"See you around," Happy said. He stepped away from the group and headed toward Big Ben and Goldi.

"See you, Happy," Reggie called.

As Happy left, he heard Cobalt say, "That Happy is a good kid. But you should stick with Reggie and me. We can tell you anything you need to know about life here."

Happy knew that Cobalt was about his age, but the handsome black horse tried to act much older sometimes.

Chapter Four

A Little Time

"Good afternoon, Happy, my boy," Big Ben said.

"Good afternoon," Happy responded. His tone was flat, and he didn't even look at Big Ben when he spoke. Happy had walked over to his friends as soon as he had left Sassafras Surprise and the other horses. He gave them both a smile. Big Ben was a jumper. Diane rode him in shows. Goldilocks had been a school pony for a long time. She usually carried the beginner riders. Happy was glad to be with Big Ben and Goldi now, but he didn't feel much like talking.

Goldi's ears flicked back as she took a bite of grass. She raised her head and looked at the younger pony. "What's the matter, Happy?"

"Aw, nothing," Happy said. He tried to sound normal, even though he knew Goldi wouldn't believe him. She always seemed to sense when something was wrong.

"Very well," Goldi answered right away. "Then why don't you eat some clover?"

"I'm not really hungry." Not even clover sounded good to Happy just then.

Goldi gave Big Ben a knowing look.

"Now, let's see, Happy," the show horse began. "This wouldn't have anything to do with the new school pony over there, would it?"

28

Happy still couldn't bring himself to look at Big Ben, but he couldn't ignore him, either. "Kind of," he admitted with a sigh. "Ivy told me to make friends with the new pony, but I don't think she really wants to be friends with me."

"What makes you say that?" Goldi asked.

"Well, she doesn't want me to call her by her nickname, for starters," Happy explained. "Everyone else is calling her Sassy, but she told me to call her Sassafras Surprise."

Goldi and Big Ben both nodded.

"And even though I offered to tell her about lessons, she said she'd ask Cobalt about being a school pony." Happy looked at his friends and decided he had said enough. He didn't want to tell them that he was also worried about Ivy liking Sassy better. That was something he would talk about with Roscoe.

"Happy," Goldi said in her kind, even way, "do you remember when you first arrived at Big Apple Barn?"

Happy had to stop himself from rolling his eyes. "Of course I do," he replied. "It wasn't that long ago."

"Do you remember how you didn't talk to me or Big Ben until you had been here for a few days?"

"Yeah," Happy said. "But that was because I didn't really know you. I didn't know that you would be so nice to me."

"Well, remember that Sassy is new. She doesn't know anyone yet, so she doesn't know who she will want to be friends with," Goldi advised. "She'll need some time to figure things out."

Happy knew Goldi was right. "Okay," he promised. "I'll give her time."

"I'm glad to hear it," Goldi said. She

stepped forward and nuzzled Happy on the cheek like his mother used to do. It made him feel better for a moment.

"That sounds like a wise plan, Happy," Big Ben said. "Time answers many questions." The noble horse gave Happy a nod of encouragement before he went back to grazing.

It *was* a wise plan, but Happy didn't want to wait. He wanted some answers right away.

He forced himself to eat a little grass. Maybe that would help him forget everything that was on his mind.

When Happy saw Diane approach the pasture, he trotted right up to the gate. He neighed good-bye to Goldilocks and Big Ben, then waited for Diane to put the lead rope on his halter.

"It seems like you're in a big hurry to come inside," Diane said to Happy. "What's the rush?"

She was right — Happy was in a hurry. He hadn't talked to Roscoe at all that day, and he wanted to see his friend. Sure enough, as soon as Diane walked him to the barn and opened the stall door, Happy spotted the mouse crouched in the back corner. Happy knew he could count on Roscoe!

"I'm so glad you're here," Happy began.

"Yeah," Roscoe replied quickly. "I'm glad you're here, too. I wanted to see what you thought of this." Roscoe held up something shiny.

"Oh," Happy said. He bent his neck down so he could inspect the object. Roscoe held it out with both hands. It was round with a hole at the top. Happy thought it must be old. "Wow," Happy said. "It looks like some kind of medal. It's very pretty."

"It is, isn't it?" Roscoe said. "Do you think Sassy would like it?"

Happy lifted his head. What did this have to do with Sassy? "I guess so," Happy answered.

"I want to give it to her," Roscoe said. "As

a welcome gift. I have some string in my nest, so I could tie it to the outside of her stall."

Happy tried to look pleased. "That would be nice of you, Roscoe."

Just then, they heard hoofbeats in the aisle. Roscoe tucked the medal under his arm and ran toward the front of the stall. He peeked under the door to get a better look. "It's her! It's Sassy!" he whispered. "See you, Happy. I have to go!"

Happy watched as the mouse ducked beneath the door and raced away. Suddenly, Happy felt very alone.

Chapter Five

A Lesson for Two

Happy was relieved when Ivy showed up at his stall the next day. It was good to see her.

"We're going to have a lesson, Happy!" Ivy announced.

Happy cocked his head to one side. It wasn't their day for a lesson. Diane had just given them one a couple of days ago, and they usually only had one lesson a week together. On other days, Happy had lessons with different riders. He always looked forward to working with Ivy most, though.

"And the best part," Ivy went on, "is that our lesson is with Andrea and Sassy."

Happy opened his eyes wide. He knew that riders often had lessons in groups, but he had only had private lessons so far — just him and his rider. Happy didn't mind a group lesson at all. He liked the idea of working with other horses and ponies. Plus, he was curious to see what Sassafras Surprise would be like with a saddle on.

Ivy grasped Happy's halter and clucked to him with her tongue. "Let's get you cleaned up, boy."

After Ivy had brushed Happy and tacked him up, they headed outside. Happy was surprised that Andrea and Sassafras Surprise were already there. Diane was sitting on the fence, looking into the riding ring.

When Diane saw Ivy and Happy, she said, "It's my two girls on Big Apple Barn's two newest ponies." Happy could tell that Diane was proud. It made him feel good. "Ivy, why don't you go ahead and get on, so we can start?"

"Okay, Mom," Ivy answered. Next, Ivy led Happy to the stair block, put her left foot in the stirrup, and pulled herself up. Happy was excited to have another lesson with Ivy. She was such a good rider. He wished she would ride him every day! She never pulled hard on his mouth with the reins, and she didn't kick too hard, either. Not all of his lesson riders were as skilled as Ivy, and none of them were as nice.

As soon as Ivy was ready, she told

Happy to walk around the ring. Out of the corner of his eye, Happy watched Sassafras Surprise. Andrea looked good on the appaloosa, but Andrea was a very talented rider. Happy guessed she looked good on most horses.

When Happy had been brand new at Big Apple Barn, Andrea was the first person to ride him. Now she was the first to ride Sassafras Surprise, too. Diane liked to see what Andrea thought of a pony before she used the pony in the riding school, so this lesson was like a test for Sassy.

"Trot on," Diane called.

Happy felt Ivy tap him with her heel. He jogged forward, stretching out his legs. Happy had a nice, long stride. He covered a lot of ground with each step, and that was a good thing. A horse or pony who could do that was called a "good mover." It was a compliment.

"She's a good mover, isn't she?" Diane said.

Happy pointed his ears toward Diane. He knew *he* was a good mover, but it sounded like Diane was talking about Sassafras Surprise.

"She is," Andrea replied. "She's a smooth ride, too."

Happy tried to lengthen his stride. He wanted them to say nice things about him!

"Happy's a good mover, too!" Ivy called.

"Why yes, he is," Diane said. "He has a lovely stride. I'm pleased with both of our new ponies."

Happy felt Ivy pat his neck. She was such a good friend. She was always looking out for him.

Next, Diane asked Ivy and Andrea to canter. After they had cantered the ponies in both directions, Diane told them to walk while she set up a fence. Happy loved jumping, and he was curious to see Sassafras Surprise go over the jump, too. So far, the new pony had done everything right. It had taken Happy a lot longer to get used to being in a new place and being ridden by a new person.

No wonder she is so sure of herself! Happy

thought. *She's beautiful, graceful, and has lots of style. If I were her, I'd be confident, too.*

Then Diane asked Andrea to trot Sassafras Surprise over the first small fence. "If she is good," Diane said, "you can take her over the rest of the course."

Andrea gathered her reins and clicked her tongue to the new pony. As Sassafras Surprise approached the fence, Happy held his breath. She bounced right over the jump, and then Andrea took her around the fences in the course. Sassafras Surprise judged every fence perfectly, lifting her front legs high every time. Happy was impressed.

"She has tons of spring!" Andrea said.

"She looks great!" Diane agreed. "Good job, Andrea. Your turn, Ivy."

Happy and Ivy went around the course. Happy listened to Ivy, and they jumped all of the fences clear. Happy was sure they looked every bit as good as Andrea and Sassafras Surprise. But when they were finished, Happy realized that Diane and Andrea had not really been watching. They were both busy petting the new pony.

Diane looked up. "Nice work, Ivy," Diane said. Then she asked Andrea to wait while she raised the fences. Happy watched with interest. He wanted to try to jump the course with the high fences. It looked exciting!

As soon as she was done setting up the course, Diane told Andrea to go ahead.

Sassafras Surprise looked just as good over the high fences. After she jumped the last one, she gave a little buck. Happy laughed to himself. He could tell the other pony was having a good time. She seemed like a lot of fun.

"I love her!" Andrea yelled. Diane smiled.

Happy stamped his foot. He couldn't wait for his turn to jump the high course! He felt Ivy shorten the reins to get ready.

"Okay, girls," Diane called, "I think that's enough for today."

"But we didn't get to go yet," Ivy said.

Diane looked at her younger daughter. "How about we try some higher fences at your next lesson?" Diane asked.

Happy heard Ivy mumble to herself. He was disappointed, too. He knew he and Ivy could jump the course. He wanted to prove it to himself — and to Sassafras Surprise.

Chapter Six

A Chat over Grass

After the lesson, Ivy and Andrea took the ponies outside on lead lines. They needed to cool them off. As the sisters walked the ponies, they talked.

"Sassy is so well-trained," Andrea said. "I think the lesson riders are going to love her."

"Yeah, she'll be good," Ivy said, glancing over at the appaloosa pony.

"You could ride her, too," Andrea suggested. "If you wanted."

Ivy sighed. Both Happy and Sassy turned to look at her. Happy didn't like the sound of this at all.

"I guess so," Ivy said. "But I like riding Happy."

Andrea looked at her little sister. "You know," she said, "you might be able to jump higher if you took your lessons on Sassy. She has so much spring! You'd like her, Ivy."

Ivy reached up and put her arm over Happy's neck. "I probably would like her," Ivy agreed. "But not as much as I like Happy. He has a lot of spring, too."

Happy felt a rush of joy. It was nice to know that Ivy liked him as much as he liked her. He just hoped that Ivy didn't change her mind.

"Okay, I won't force you," Andrea insisted, putting up her hand. "It was just an idea. I think the ponies are cooled off now," she said, changing the subject. "Do you want to let them eat some grass?"

Oh! Happy thought. *It would be nice to have some grass before dinner.* Happy and Sassafras Surprise looked at each other. Happy could tell that the other pony agreed. They followed the girls to a patch of tall, thick grass close to the ring. Andrea and Ivy sat down, leaning against the side of the barn.

The ponies immediately thrust their heads toward the ground. But before they reached the grass, their noses bumped together.

"Oh, sorry," Happy said. He pulled his head up and looked away, embarrassed.

"It was my fault," Sassafras Surprise replied. "Please, after you."

"No," Happy said. "You know, ladies first and all that."

Sassafras Surprise let out a light nickering laugh. "Very funny," she said. "I think there's plenty for both of us. But I like meeting a pony with a sense of humor." She paused for a moment and then lowered her neck to take a bite. "It's quite good. You should have some."

Happy took a step to the side and then plunged his muzzle into the sweet, grassy goodness. Even though he didn't get to jump the higher round of fences, he had still worked up an appetite! As he ate, he thought about Sassafras Surprise. He remembered that Goldi and Big Ben said he should give her some time to get used to her new home, but he thought this was a good chance to get to know her better.

"So, Sassafras Surprise —"

"Please, call me Sassy," the pony said.

Happy nodded. He was glad to be able to call her by her nickname. It was a good sign that they were getting along. "So, Sassy, do you like it at Big Apple Barn?" he asked.

The young pony lifted her head. She finished chewing before she spoke. "I like it well enough." Her speech was polished, yet she seemed relaxed. "Everyone is nice."

Happy thought she was easier to talk to now than when she had been in the field with the other horses. "That's good," Happy replied. Happy searched for what to say next. He knew that Cobalt had offered to talk to her about being a school pony, but Cobalt wasn't around. And Sassy had just finished her first lesson, so the timing seemed good. "Do you have any questions about being a school pony?"

Sassy took a short breath. Happy saw a spark in her eyes as she lifted her head.

"Well, if today is any example," she began, "I would say that I've already mastered that, wouldn't you?"

Happy was shocked. Suddenly, Sassy sounded like a different pony. She sounded very sure of herself again — confident. A little *too* confident.

Happy didn't know what to say. He did know that being ridden by Andrea was much different than being ridden by a lesson rider. Andrea was very good. She knew just what to do to make a pony understand her. The riding-school students were just learning. He thought he should try to explain that. But when Happy looked at Sassy, he lost his nerve. He didn't think he could tell her something like that. Besides, he wasn't sure she would want to listen.

"You looked great," Happy said instead.

"Why, thank you," Sassy responded. "You looked pretty good yourself." She gave Happy a smile.

Happy smiled halfheartedly in return. It was true. Sassy *had* looked great. He just didn't think her lesson with Andrea was proof that she would definitely be a great school pony.

Chapter Seven

The Deep, Dark Woods

"Hey, Roscoe," Happy called as the mouse rushed by his stall. Happy hadn't seen his friend at all the day before. He wondered why the mouse had not come to visit.

"Oh, hey, Happy." Roscoe looked up and down the barn aisle before walking over to Happy's stall.

"I missed you yesterday," Happy said.

Roscoe let out a short sigh. "Yeah, I was

kind of busy. Sassy had some extra grain in her stall, so I helped her get rid of it."

"That sounds good," Happy said. He knew how much his friend liked grain.

"I did my corn-tooth joke for her," Roscoe said, grinning.

"Oh, that's nice," Happy said. Roscoe liked to put two pieces of yellow corn in front of his teeth to make the horses and ponies laugh. It was a pretty funny joke. "That's one of my favorites," Happy added. "I bet Sassy liked it."

"Yeah, she did," Roscoe said. "Speaking of Sassy, did you talk to her yesterday?"

"Um . . ." Happy looked at his friend. He wasn't sure why Roscoe would be asking him that question. "Yeah, we talked after our lesson."

"Well, did you talk *about* your lesson?" Roscoe said.

"A little, I guess," Happy answered.

"Why did you do that?" Roscoe put his hands on his hips. "I thought I told you she was nervous about being a school pony. You shouldn't have brought it up."

Happy shook his head. "I didn't know what else to say," he explained. "I was just trying to be friendly."

"Well, if you were a real friend, you wouldn't bring up things that make her nervous," Roscoe said.

Happy thought about that. Sassy had not seemed nervous about being a school pony. If anything, she had seemed the exact opposite. "She didn't seem worried at all."

"Well, that's not what she told me," Roscoe insisted. "Maybe you should just mind your own business and leave her alone." Without another word, the mouse stormed off, whipping his tail behind him.

Happy was shocked. Why was Roscoe so upset? He and Roscoe had never argued before, and Happy didn't think he had done anything wrong. He put his head over his stall door, wanting to call out after the mouse. But then he saw Ivy striding toward him.

"Guess what, Happy," Ivy prompted. "Mom says we can go on a trail ride."

A trail ride? Happy had never been on one of those. Ivy made it sound like fun, and he was happy to have something to take his mind off of Sassy and Roscoe. He thought a trail ride would be just the thing.

After Ivy tacked Happy up, she took him to the outdoor ring. Once she had climbed up into the saddle, she guided Happy out of the ring through the gate. They walked along a path next to the pasture. *This is new,* Happy thought. He had never gone beyond the field.

"Let's go into the woods," Ivy said. Happy flicked back one of his ears so he could hear Ivy better. "There's a nice trail through there." Ivy pointed.

Happy turned his head slightly and looked into the woods. They were deep and dark. The trees grew tall and close together. Happy didn't really want to follow that trail, but he trusted Ivy. Ivy tugged lightly on the reins, and Happy took the path under the tree branches. He blinked as his eyes became used to the shadowy trail. He pricked his ears forward.

"It's okay, boy," Ivy reassured Happy,

giving him a pat. "It just seems spooky at first."

Happy took a deep breath. If Ivy said it was safe, he believed her. As they walked deeper into the forest, Happy began to relax. He decided that the woods were actually quite pretty. Everything had a green glow. The sunlight broke through the branches, shining like sparkly jewels.

"I love it out here," Ivy said. "It's so quiet."

Happy listened. All he could hear was the wind in the trees and the calls of birds. Happy decided he liked it in the woods, too. He was glad Ivy had brought him here. He never would have been brave enough to explore it on his own.

"Happy?" Ivy asked, pausing until she had the pony's attention. Happy flicked his ear back and waited for her to say more. "Thanks for making friends with Sassy. I know it's hard to be new, and she could use a good friend like you."

As he walked, Happy thought about Ivy's words. It had seemed like he was on his way to being friends with the new pony. She had told him he could call her Sassy. He treated her nicely. He had even tried to give her advice about being a school pony, but she had not wanted it. But from what Roscoe had said, Happy had upset Sassy. It didn't really make sense.

Happy remembered how when Sassy first arrived, he had been worried that Ivy would want to ride her. He had wanted to talk to Roscoe about it and everything. But now he and Ivy were still close. Instead, it was Roscoe who seemed to be becoming buddies with the new pony. He hadn't thought anything would ever come between him and Roscoe. They had been through so much together!

Happy had to figure out how to make things right. Right with Sassy, and right with Roscoe, too.

Chapter Eight

Some Bad Luck

A few days had passed, and Happy was enjoying an afternoon in the field with his friends. Everyone was there — Goldi, Big Ben, Cobalt, Reggie. Well, almost everyone.

Roscoe was missing. Of course, Roscoe was a mouse, so he didn't get turned out in the field. But Happy hadn't seen Roscoe in the barn lately, either. Things felt weird without Roscoe around. Happy had not talked to the mouse for two days. Roscoe seemed to be avoiding him. Happy wasn't sure what he had done wrong. He just knew that he missed his friend.

Sassy wasn't in the field, either, but Happy knew why. She was going to have her first lesson as a school pony that day.

Before long, Happy saw Diane walk out of the barn. She was with a young girl, and the girl was leading Sassy. Happy had never seen the girl. He guessed she might be a new student.

"So you've taken lessons before?" Diane asked.

"Uh-huh, lots," the girl replied. "At another barn."

"Okay then," Diane said. "How about you get on and walk Sassy around the ring?"

Happy didn't want to spy on Sassy's first lesson, but he couldn't help watching. It would be impossible to just ignore her. The ring was right next to the pasture!

Goldi stepped up beside Happy. "Not too long ago, that was you," the older pony said.

"I know." Happy looked at his friend. "I was so nervous during my first lesson."

"I remember," Goldi admitted. "I'm sure Sassy is, too."

"Really?" Happy asked. "But she was so good when Andrea rode her."

"Now, Happy," Goldi said. "You know that being ridden by Andrea is not like being a school pony."

Happy did know that. Suddenly, he was worried about Sassy. She really didn't know what being a school pony was all about.

Happy saw that things started to go wrong

as soon as the lesson began. When Diane told Sassy's rider to ask for a trot, the rider bounced up and down in the saddle. Happy knew that riders usually moved up and down during the trot. It was called posting, and it helped to make the trot more comfortable for both the horse and the rider. But this lesson student was not posting well. She was hitting the saddle too hard. Happy knew it must hurt Sassy's back. The pony's ears were pinned back, and she looked upset.

"Things don't look like they are going well for Sassy," Happy said to Goldi.

"No, they don't," Goldi agreed. "It's bad luck that she didn't get a better rider for her first lesson. But Diane can tell the rider what to do." It was Diane's job to teach her students to become better riders. Happy hoped Diane would be able to help.

"Tighten your legs around Sassy. Press them against the saddle," Diane called from her seat in the center of the ring. "It will make posting easier. Then her trot will feel nice and smooth."

Goldi and Happy watched, but it didn't look like the rider was getting better. Her legs were loose, and they kept flopping against Sassy's sides. As the rider bounced up and down, Sassy sped up. Now the rider was hitting the saddle harder, and her legs were still jabbing into Sassy's belly.

"She's going too fast for me!" the rider complained.

Happy flinched as he watched. "It's not Sassy's fault!" Happy said to Goldi. "Look at how the rider is kicking her! Sassy thinks she's supposed to go faster."

Goldi nodded in agreement.

"Sit back in the saddle and tighten your

64

reins!" Diane yelled. She then stood up and walked toward the pony and rider.

The rider flopped forward in the saddle. She was losing control! Sassy kept trotting at full speed. Happy held his breath. He knew Sassy wasn't sure what to do, so she just kept going.

"Pull back on the reins!" Diane called again, and rushed toward Sassy, trying to catch up to the frightened pony. All of a sudden, the rider caught her balance. She sat back and yanked on the reins. When Sassy felt the jerk of the reins, her head flew up. She locked her legs in place and jolted to a stop. She was breathing hard, and the whites of her eyes flashed in fear.

"I hate this pony!" the rider wailed. She threw the reins from her hands and fumbled out of the saddle. When her feet hit the ground, she turned toward Diane, who was already running over. "This pony doesn't listen at all!"

Happy couldn't believe it. "But Sassy did just what the rider asked her to do!" he insisted to Goldi. He had seen how the rider kept kicking Sassy, and she had not pulled on the reins to tell Sassy to slow down.

"I know," Goldi said. "The rider just wasn't

able to tell Sassy what she wanted. Let's hope Diane can make things better."

"I want to ride another pony!" the rider yelled.

Happy saw Sassy look at her rider. The new pony was bewildered. She snorted and began to back away.

Before Diane was able to do anything, Sassy spun around. With a burst of speed, Sassy darted toward the other end of the ring. Her reins dragged on the ground, and her stirrups slapped against her sides. When she reached the entrance to the ring, she ran through the open gate. Her hooves thudded against the hard ground as she galloped past the field.

Happy gasped. Sassy was headed straight for the deep, dark woods.

Chapter Nine

The Rescue

"What do we do?" Happy asked. He looked toward the woods, but Sassy had already disappeared into the thick growth of trees.

"We wait," said Big Ben, turning to Happy. "We wait for Sassy to come back."

All of the horses in the field were gathered together. They were talking about what had happened to Sassafras Surprise during her lesson. She had seemed so upset, and they all understood why.

"Diane will probably go after her, don't you think?" Goldi asked, her voice hopeful.

"She'd better," Cobalt said. "She shouldn't have put that rider on Sassy in the first place. The girl obviously was not very good."

"Diane didn't know," Goldi insisted. "The rider was new here, but she'd taken lessons somewhere else."

Happy looked toward the barn. Diane was upset that Sassy had run off, too. He could tell. But Happy wasn't worried about Diane. He was worried about Sassy.

He realized that Roscoe had been right. Sassy had seemed very confident about being a school pony after her lesson with Andrea. But she wasn't. She had been nervous all along.

"We can't just stand here," Happy said. "Those woods can be scary, and Sassy is all alone." Happy remembered how spooky the forest had seemed at first, and he thought of the look in Sassy's eyes as she had galloped off. "What if she doesn't come back?"

"There's nothing we can do," Cobalt declared. "Sassy was smart to run away. Now Diane knows she means business. She'll come back sooner or later."

But Happy wasn't so sure. Sassy had not taken off into the woods to prove a point. She had been frightened and uncertain. She needed to talk to someone. Happy knew there *was* something he could do. He looked at the pasture fence, then he looked at the other horses. He knew he shouldn't do what he was thinking. But if they weren't going to help Sassy, he would.

"I'm going after her," Happy said. "I'll be back as soon as I can." Without waiting for a response, Happy started to canter toward the fence. It was a tall fence, but Happy knew he could jump really high — even higher without a rider. He was sure he could clear it.

"Happy, no!"

Happy could hear Goldi call to him, but he did not slow down. He knew what he needed to do. He lengthened his stride. He aimed for the shortest part of the fence. With a mighty leap, he soared over the

wooden rails. Once he landed on the other side, he didn't look back. He ran right into the woods in search of Sassy.

Happy followed the trail that he and Ivy had ridden on. "Sassy!" he called. "It's me, Happy." He walked quickly, scanning the path. The woods were dark with shadows, but Happy wasn't scared. He just wanted to find Sassy.

"Sassy! Where are you?" Happy yelled. He wondered how far she might have gone. The woods were big and deep. She could be anywhere. And, if she didn't want Happy to find her, she could hide.

Happy walked farther and farther into the woods. The farther he went, the darker it became. The wind whipped through the trees and the leaves trembled, but Happy kept going. He walked for a long time. Just when he thought he might be lost, he saw something shift in the shadows. It was a big bush, and it looked like it was moving.

"Sassy?" Happy said. He walked toward the bush. "Sassy, is that you?"

The leaves of the bush quivered. "No," the bush said. "I don't know anyone named Sassy."

Happy rolled his eyes. "Come on, Sassy," he insisted. "I know it's you."

"I don't want to talk about it," Sassy said.

"You don't have to talk about it," Happy reassured her. "But everyone back at Big Apple Barn is worried about you. We want you to come home."

The leaves of the bush rustled, and Sassy poked her head out. "Let's be honest, Happy. I don't really have a home," Sassy said. "Big Apple Barn is for school ponies. I don't belong there. I'm a horrible school pony! I knew I would be."

"You were *not* horrible," Happy told her. "That rider was not very good, and you just tried to do what she asked. Every rider is different, and she wasn't a good match for you."

"But then I'm not made to be a school pony," Sassy said. "I was never that confused with my old owner, or with Andrea."

"It's not your fault, Sassy," Happy told her. "You didn't know what to expect." Happy took a breath and looked off in the direction of Big Apple Barn. "I know it's probably none of my business, but . . . you could have asked me."

Sassy took a few steps out from

behind the bush, then paused. "I could have.

But Roscoe told me how you are Diane's favorite school pony. And how smart you are." Sassy looked down at the ground. "So when I met you, I wanted you to think good things about me. I didn't want to admit that I didn't understand what being a school pony is all about."

"Did Roscoe really say all that? He shouldn't have," Happy told her. He was surprised to hear what Sassy had to say. "You don't have to act like you know things you don't. I didn't know anything about lessons when I started. And I'm still new, too. I make lots of mistakes." It was true. He gave Sassy his most encouraging smile. "It takes time to learn to be a school pony. Just like it takes time to make real friends."

Sassy stared down at her hooves. "So we're friends?" she asked.

"Friends," Happy agreed with a nod of his

head. "And if, as friends, you ever want to talk about something, maybe like how to be a school pony, just let me know."

"That would be nice, Happy," Sassy said with a sigh. "But what if it's too late? Will Diane really take me back?"

"Well, there's one way to find out," Happy announced. "Let's head back to Big Apple Barn."

With that, the two ponies turned and set off down the trail, walking side by side.

Chapter Ten

Home at Last

When Happy and Sassy came out of the woods, Goldilocks, Cobalt, and Reggie were all waiting.

"Thank goodness you are both all right!" Goldi cried.

"Diane is busy tacking up Big Ben right now. She was starting a search party," Cobalt said. "She was really worried, Sassy."

"Oh!" Sassy began. "I didn't mean to

upset anyone. I was so confused. I just needed to get away." The appaloosa dropped her head.

"Now, Sassy," Goldi said. "There's nothing to be ashamed of. You're a good pony. Diane knows that. She feels just awful." Then Goldi glanced over at Happy. "And Happy, Ivy is beside herself with worry over you," she added. "You should never have left the pasture on your own." Goldi gave Happy a long, hard look. Happy couldn't meet her eyes.

"But it was pretty cool when you jumped the fence," Reggie said with a laugh. Reggie and Cobalt nodded to each other, but Goldi frowned. She was only half the size of the two younger horses, yet it was obvious who was in charge.

"You two get inside," Goldi advised, turning back to Happy and Sassy. "They'll be so glad to see you. We're all relieved to have you back safe."

Happy and Sassy walked along the path toward the stables. As they neared the big barn doors, Sassy slowed down. "Happy?" she said.

Happy paused and looked back at the new pony.

"I'm nervous," Sassy admitted.

"That's okay," Happy said. "I'm nervous, too. But at least we're together."

"Mom!" They heard a voice yell. "They came back!" Then Happy heard a rush of footsteps. Suddenly, Ivy was there, and she wrapped her arms around Happy's neck.

"Oh, Happy, I'm so glad you came back!" Ivy exclaimed. "And you brought Sassy." Ivy let go of Happy and gave Sassy a kiss on the cheek. "Mom was so worried! Sassy, she feels really bad."

"What a relief!" Diane said, hurrying down the aisle toward them. When she reached the ponies, she touched each one on the muzzle.

Andrea came up behind her. "I guess we can cancel the search party," she said. "Happy is a hero. I can't believe he jumped out of the pasture to follow Sassy! You were right, Ivy. Happy does have a lot of spring."

"I normally would be far from pleased that a pony jumped out of the field," Diane said. "But this is a special situation. In this case, Happy Go Lucky, I agree that you're a hero." She smiled. "And a good friend."

"The best," Ivy agreed, scratching Happy behind the ears.

"Oh, Sassy," Diane said. "I hope you can

forgive me. I should have realized that rider wasn't good enough to ride you yet. Don't worry. We have lots of riders who will be a good match for you. You'll be a wonderful school pony."

Sassy looked up at Diane. The new pony seemed pleased.

"She will be great," Andrea said. "She just needs a little time, like Happy did."

Happy looked at his friend, and Sassy smiled at him.

"Let's get the saddle and bridle off of Sassy," Diane suggested. "She's probably tired and sore."

Andrea took Sassy by the reins and led her down the aisle. "Sassy, we'll give you a good brushing and some warm bran mash," Andrea said. "Then you'll feel as good as new."

"Same for you, Happy," Ivy said. "You just wait in your stall, and I'll get your brushes."

When Happy stepped into his stall, he was surprised to see Roscoe sitting in his favorite spot near the back wall. "Hello, Happy," the mouse said in a quiet voice.

"Hi, Roscoe," Happy replied.

"I'm glad you're back. I felt so bad when I heard you followed Sassy," Roscoe said. His brown eyes were big and sincere. "I guess you did know what she needed from a friend."

"She just needed someone to talk to," Happy said. "We all need that sometimes, right?"

"Right," Roscoe said, nodding and looking sheepish. "I think I just wanted to be her friend, and I wanted to be your friend. But I didn't really want you to be friends with each other."

Happy was impressed that Roscoe was being so honest with him. "Roscoe, you know we're friends. You've been my best pal since I got here."

"I know. But I was afraid that if you had a fun pony friend, you wouldn't need me." Roscoe kicked at a piece of straw with his back leg.

"I'll still need you," Happy said. "I promise."

Roscoe looked at Happy with searching eyes.

"I mean," Happy continued, "who else would do the corn-tooth joke for me when I'm feeling down?"

"I *am* funny," Roscoe said, smiling.

"And who would tell me all the news about what's happening around the barn?" Happy asked.

"That's one of my special talents," Roscoe admitted.

"Yeah," Happy agreed. Then he paused for a moment, so he knew Roscoe was really listening. "And even if it weren't for that, I would still want you for a friend. No one could replace you."

"Really?" The mouse looked Happy in the eye. "So we're still friends?"

"We're still friends," Happy said, nodding.

"And you and Sassy are friends," Roscoe said. "So we can all be friends."

"Sure enough," Happy said.

Then Happy's stall door opened, and Ivy walked in. Roscoe tried to scamper away, but Ivy saw him.

"Oh, look! A mouse!" she whispered to herself. "Happy, is this your friend?" Ivy bent down on her knees. "Hey, little fellow. Do you want a treat?" Ivy reached into her pocket and pulled out a piece of carrot. "Any friend of Happy's is a friend of mine," Ivy said. She held the carrot out in her hand.

Roscoe looked at Happy, and the pony nodded. Then Roscoe creeped forward and lifted the carrot from Ivy's fingers.

Happy smiled. If Roscoe was willing to share Sassy, Happy was willing to share Ivy. That was a great thing about Big Apple Barn. It *was* big. And there was plenty of friendship to go around.

Learn your way around
BIG APPLE BARN!

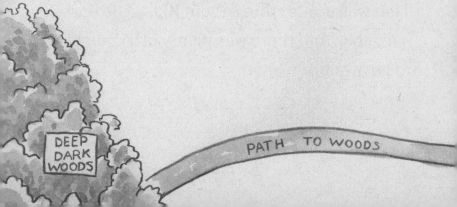

About the Author

Kristin Earhart grew up in Worthington, Ohio, where she spent countless waking and sleeping hours dreaming about horses and ponies. She started riding lessons at eight, and her trainer really was named Diane. Kristin's pony, Moochie, and her horse, Wendy, were two of the best friends a girl could have. As is her husband. They live in Brooklyn, New York, with their son.

A magical adventure begins...

Rainbow Magic #1: Ruby the Red Fairy
by Daisy Meadows

When Rachel and Kirsty arrive at Rainspell Island for vacation, they are in for a big surprise! The seven Rainbow Fairies have been banished from fairyland by the wicked Jack Frost. If they don't return soon, Fairyland is doomed to be colorless and gray!

In the pot at the end of the rainbow, Rachel and Kirsty discover Ruby the Red Fairy. Can they keep her safe and find the rest of her Rainbow sisters...before it's too late?

SCHOLASTIC

www.scholastic.com

Rain or Shine, It's Fairy Time

The Weather Fairies

RAINBOW magic
THE WEATHER FAIRIES

Crystal
the Snow
Fairy

by Daisy Meadows

■ SCHOLASTIC

Crystal the Snow Fairy has lost her magic weather feather, and now it's snowing in summer! Can Rachel and Kirsty find the feather and fix the weather in Fairyland?

■ SCHOLASTIC